Evincepub Publishing

Parijat Extension, Bilaspur, Chhattisgarh 495001
First Published By Evincepub Publishing 2021
Copyright © Jharna Mehta, Hira Mehta 2021
All Rights Reserved.

ISBN: 978-93-5446-035-7

TALES OF FRIENDSHIP

AGE 6+

Jharna Mehta

Hira Mehta

DEDICATED TO

My son, Kian,
nephew, Aarav
and niece, Ayanna.
Grateful for the love of Dad and Mom
Pratik Bhai and Suman Bhabhi
my Mini Kaki and Nishita Ben.
A big thank you to Dhaivat Kaka
for all the fun stories he told me in my
childhood and continues to tell even today
that inspired me to write this book.

~ Jharna

My grandkids,
Kian,
Aarav
and Ayanna.
Grateful for the love and support of
Chintan, Suman, Pratik, Nishita
Dhun, Ruby and Damini.

~ Hira

Thank you for always being there for us

Authors Note

This is a short story collection titled "*Tales of Friendship - Age 6+*". We are a daughter-mother duo and the story ideas are all mine. We hope you like what we have put together for you. Friendships matter and we all know how much it means to have a friend. These stories will show that in the end there is always hope and a way out when you have friends. I have also attempted to illustrate the book for the first time and I hope you like it.

Jharna Mehta

Believe me when I say that we brainstormed a lot. Oh yes, like all mothers and daughters do, we argued a lot about the way the story should go. These delightful stories, conjured up by Jharna, that we have written together are fun adventures of friendships to fire up your imagination and fill you with a sense of wonder. We are sure you will enjoy reading them as much as much as we enjoyed writing them for you.

Hira Mehta

Contents

ILLUSTRATIONS BY JHARNA MEHTA

1

THE JEALOUS CAMEL AND THE LEOPARD

The camel in this story lived in a zoo at the edge of the town. The zoo was a lively place with large cages of animals and birds. There were leopards, elephants, camels, snakes, and a hippopotamus too. Children were running around happily. People were feeding the ducks and swans swimming in the beautiful lake. The duck turned up its nose at the monkey in the cage next to the lake. The monkey was busy playing on an old tire hung from the top of the cage. His cage was next to the camel. He stuck his tongue out at the camel. The camel turned away and chewed on the grass. In the small cage next to the camel there lived a very lazy leopard. He laughed at the camel chewing on the grass.

The leopard got all the attention from the children and no one came near the camel's cage. This made the camel very jealous. "I have to get him to move from here. He is very annoying and noisy," he thought. He made a plan.

He threw grass at him to make his cage dirty, but the leopard happily made a bed out of it and went to sleep. When the plan failed, the camel made another plan. He threw water in his cage, but the wily leopard rolled around in the water and enjoyed it because he was feeling hot.

The camel thought to himself, "Ok, let me try one final plan. Let me tease him." He teased the leopard by making noises throughout the night, but it did not work. The leopard teased him back so, finally, he gave up.

Fed-up, the camel called out to the leopard and said, "Who do you think you are showing off to the children like that?" The leopard replied, "I am an animal."

The camel said, "So you think you are very funny. I tried so many things to get you angry, but how come you did not react."

The leopard said, "I am not like you. I could see you doing bad things, but do you think my life is easy? My life is even worse than yours. You are allowed to roam in your cage, but not me. I want to sleep on the tree branch, but every night I am locked up in the small cage at the back with one bowl of water. Children don't love me. They just come to stare and make fun of me, asking me to growl. I also get dragged to have baths daily and you know that cats don't like getting wet. We just lick ourselves clean."

The camel felt ashamed hearing this and replied, "I am so sorry. I did not know. I have been jealous of you, because no one cares about me either. I hate it here. There is no sand for me to sleep on. I hate giving rides around the zoo to people. It makes me dizzy going round and round along the same path. I guess we both are unhappy and no one will ever care about us. Maybe we can be friends."

They became friends, but it was too late. People who had visited the zoo complained to the zookeeper that the camel had turned mad. They said he was throwing things at the leopard and going round and round in circles. The zookeeper came and moved the camel to another cage.

This made the camel very sad and he realized that by troubling another, he had put himself in trouble. He missed his friend, but the camel now began to enjoy the rides he gave to people. He made it a point to stop near the leopard's cage and say hello to his friend, refusing to move for a long time.

The zookeeper was surprised and people would stand near the leopard's cage to see the funny sight. The loud rumbling, grunting and roars of the two soon became the talk of the town. It was not long before the camel was moved back to be close to his friend.

Moral: Be aware of your surroundings first and understand what someone else's life is like before hurting another person.

2

THE LOST CROCODILE

Once there was a baby crocodile called Croaky. He was dark green, with a long tail, and lived on the banks of a beautiful river close to the forest. Croaky loved the dark river with its green trees and ice-cream-shaped boulders. It was a place where he felt peaceful. Croaky loved to splash about in the cold water and swim back and forth.

When he got tired, he would climb onto the floating logs and sleep. When the sunset over the mountains, his mother would call out to him to get off the log and come home. That day, he pretended not to hear her. He closed his eyes and the water rocked him to sleep. The log gently floated along the river. Mrs. Trout splashed around the water daring him to catch her, but Croaky turned his nose up at her and went right back to sleep.

The sound of the waterfall woke him up. Everything around him looked different. He tried to make sense of his surroundings. He knew now that he was lost. He jumped into the water, crawled onto the land and ran into the forest. He saw a dark cave ahead but

Croaky thought to himself, "I should have stayed near the water. Oh, why did I run? I don't like dark caves. I am not going into that cave and I don't think I should go any further. Oh my! What am I going to do?" It was getting dark. He knew he would get lost in the dark, so scared Croaky stopped under a tree. "Hello, is anyone there? I don't know my way back home. Can someone please help me!" he cried.

He peered into the darkness and thought he saw something move. All of a sudden, he heard a crow cawing from high up above in the tree's branches. Croaky called out for help.

On the tree lived Mr. Owl who was trying to sleep. Hearing the cry for help, he got up and peeped out from among the leaves just as Mrs. Crow flew down and sat on a rock far away from Croaky.

Croaky said, "I won't hurt you. I am just a baby, so please could you help me find my way back to the water."

Mr. Owl asked, "Where did you come from?" Croaky said, "I floated down the river on a log and I am lost now."

"Oh, dear. Let me help you get home through the forest since I can see clearly in the dark. Just follow the cawing of my friend, Mrs. Crow," Mr. Owl said.

Croaky asked, "Can I just not swim back? I am not comfortable walking."

Mrs. Crow smiled and said, "We would be happy to help but we can't swim. So let's just try it our way. Mr. Owl will fly above the trees and I will fly low and caw so you can hear my voice and follow me."

So Mr. Owl flew off first and then Mrs. Crow followed him cawing loudly. Croaky followed the sound of Mrs. Crow. Mrs. Crow soon got tired of cawing.

"Stop. Stop please, Mr. Owl." screamed Mrs. Crow, "I am tired of cawing. My mouth hurts, so can we stop for a while". They stopped to perch over the branches as Mrs. Crow caught her breath. Soon they were off on their way again. "Caw, Caw, Caw," went Mrs. Crow in the silence of the dark night.

Suddenly, Mrs. Crow realized that there was no noise from behind, so she turned and saw that Croaky was not there. Thinking that he must have flown too fast and Croaky must have been left behind, she told Mr. Owl to stop flying. They turned back to look for him. Some time passed in searching for him in the dark forest when suddenly they heard a cry for help. It was Croaky. His leg was stuck in a rope in the mud. Mrs. Crow flew down onto his back and nipped off the rope.

Nip, Nip, Nip went Mrs. Crow. "There, it is done. Now push yourself out," Mr. Owl hooted loudly. The grateful Croaky pushed himself out of the mud and they continued their journey.

"I hope you know where you are taking me" said Croaky.

"Don't worry, "replied Mr. Owl, "It is the same river you floated along and we are going in the direction you came from. You said your home is close to the huge boulders that look like ice-cream cones. I will find it."

The forest was silent and the only sound heard was that of the cawing of the crow and the rustling of the crocodile through the leaves. "Stop, stop, I am tired and hungry from walking. You know crocodiles are meant to swim and not walk in the forest," Croaky said panting. They stopped under a big dark tree and Mrs. Crow flew around to find food.

"Come quickly. This way," shouted Mrs. Crow. The three of them looked up at the beautiful jackfruit tree.

"How are we going to get the jackfruit to fall for Croaky to eat," asked Mr. Owl, "it is too big and heavy for us to break."

"I will do it," said Croaky and with the help of his large tail, he banged the tree trunk again and again till the jackfruit fell on the ground.

The three friends ate the jackfruit till they could eat no more. Then they were off again on their journey.

"There, there, I can see your home," said Mr. Owl. "Go to your left Croaky and follow the path."

Croaky smiled and scampered as fast as he could. He jumped into the water and screamed with joy upon seeing his worried mother. He went round and round in the water, happy to be home. Mr. Owl and Mrs. Crow sat down on a rock and laughed.

"If you had not helped my son, he would have been lost forever in the dark forest. Don't go back. Stay on the trees here and live with us," said Mrs. Crocodile thanking them for having saved her son.

Croaky was soon back to sleeping on the logs floating in the river. He knew he could sleep peacefully and float around. He now had Mrs. Crow and Mr. Owl sitting on the log with him. Croaky knew that he would never get lost again as he had his friends to guide him back home.

Moral: Sometimes it takes an adventure to get you to meet the right kind of friends.

3

THE OWL THAT FELL FROM THE TREE

Long ago in a forest, with many beautiful trees, at the edge of the green path leading to the caves in the distance, stood a big and strong banyan tree. On this tree, there lived an Owl. He was called Darko. Darko would sleep from morning till night and wake up when the moon came up in the sky. He would then hoot and hoot through the night, guarding his friend who lived under the tree. A baby elephant who had no mother. His mother had left him long ago. So Darko had named the elephant, Fatso.

The baby elephant never asked why he was named Fatso because he knew he was very fat. He loved his friend very much. Fatso loved to shake the tree with his strong trunk. Darko didn't mind him shaking the tree while he was asleep in the daytime. It felt like he was rocking in a cradle.

It was the middle of the afternoon. Fatso was bored and not feeling sleepy. He forgot that Darko had hurt his wing and was sleeping. He started to shake the tree so hard that Darko lost his balance. He tried to grab the branch, but because his wing was hurt, he fell and bumped his head.

Darko started to cry, "Ouch my wing. Ouch my head too," and fainted.

Fatso picked him up with his trunk, cuddled him and said, "Oh my, what have I done. I told you to let me take you to the animal doctor in the village when you hurt your wing. You could have flown off if your wing was fine. It is all my fault now."

Holding Darko gently, Fatso ran for help. He ran as fast as he could down the dark path with thick dark green branches arching over. He even crossed a lion's den and when he heard the lion roar, he ran even faster. He knew that he had to get his friend to the animal doctor as fast as he could.

Fatso suddenly stopped. He saw a small boy with a goat. The boy was plucking leaves from a plant. It was Kian, and Gonso the goat. They looked at him frightened.

Fatso said, "Don't be frightened. I know you. You are the doctor's son. Please help me. My friend is hurt and it is all my fault."

Kian smiled, "Let me help you. I know a little about medicine and I have a few in my bag."

Fatso slowly put Darko down on the ground and Kian quickly took out a bottle and applied medicine on Darko's head. Darko was still unconscious and didn't know what was happening. They waited for

Darko to open his eyes. They heard a lion roar in the distance.

Darko suddenly woke up and asked, with one eye closed, "Where did that noise come from? Is that the lion I hear? I think the lion is hurt."

Gonso asked, "How do you know he is hurt? Fatso, do you remember passing a lion's den?"

Fatso said, "Yes, I did."

Gonso was very scared upon hearing this. Gonso shivered in fright and pulled Kian by his shirt, and said, "Kian, come on, it is getting dark. Let us go home before the lion comes."

Darko stopped them and said, "Don't be silly. The lion is not going to come here." Just as he had said this, a huge lion came roaring out of the bushes and they all trembled with fear.

Mr. Lion roared and then went, "Ouch, Ouch. I have something stuck in my tooth. I have not eaten for days," and sat down, groaning in pain.

"Not eaten for days. Oh my, he is going to eat us all," cried Gonso.

Mr. Lion came close to Gonso and looked him in the eye and said angrily, "I will eat you first if you do not help me."

"I think Kian should help Mr. Lion. He helped me did he not," said Darko.

Gonso got angry and said, "Why should we help? My family was eaten up by lions so I don't like all lions. It was Kian who saved me and took good care of me."

Mr. Lion looked at Gonso and snarled. Kian said, "Please, please, Mr. Lion, leave him alone. He is just angry and hurt." He turned to Gonso, "I understand what you are feeling, Gonso, but I have got to help.

My father will be very disappointed if I do not. He always helps all animals." Kian asked the lion what was hurting him.

Mr. Lion replied, "I don't know, but something seems to be stuck in my tooth and it is hurting me.

Please help me. I won't eat you, I promise."

Kian went close to the lion and saw small thread stuck in his tooth. He said, "Darko, sit on the lion's nose and pull it out."

So Darko sat on the lion's nose and peeped into his mouth. Mr. Lion roared with pain as Darko pulled the string out. Kian gently applied the medicine to the tooth and in no time Mr. Lion felt better.

Mr. Lion sighed in relief and smiled wickedly, "Now I am going to eat you all up."

Fatso caught his tail and said, "No way. You are not hurting my friends."

"Ouch, ouch, let go of my tail," said Mr. Lion, "I was only teasing you all. I want to be your friend. Dear Gonso, I am so sorry that lions killed your family. I promise I will never harm you. Will you be my friend?"

Gonso smiled and began to dance and they all burst out laughing.

Mr. Lion turned to Fatso and said, "Fatso, I hope you have learned your lesson. When someone dear to you is hurt or sleeping, you should not trouble them just for fun. I know it was an accident, but you have to be careful."

Then he turned to Darko, "Please show us the way home." Darko started to sing,

"Together let's run
Come on everyone
You too naughty Fatso
It's time for us to go
Run behind me in a line
We will reach home in no time."

Moral: Do not trouble others and help even your enemies. No matter how small you are, you can still help others.

4

THE UNHAPPY LAMB

Once on a beautiful farm, there lived a girl and her name was Esha. She had a pet lamb who was pink in colour and his name was Limbo. Limbo had a black mark in the shape of a heart on his forehead. Esha kept him in the house with her and never allowed Limbo to play with the other lambs in the barn. Limbo hated being in the house the whole day.

He thought to himself, "Why did Esha snatch me away from my flock? Why can't she understand that I want to be with my family?"

Esha never understood how much he missed his family and his twin brother, Larky. Limbo remembered bleating in sorrow when Esha picked him up saying, "Dad, I want this one as a pet," and carried him off into the house. It had been many months now and she never allowed him to leave the house.

Esha took good care of him but Limbo was very unhappy. Limbo wanted to be with Larky and the other baby lambs. He stood up on his hind legs at the window and watched the other lambs playing in the barn. Esha was busy cooking. He bleated and bleated but she told him to be quiet. He knew now that he would have to run away. He waited for her to open the door and sneaked out between her legs when she was not looking.

Larky screamed with joy as his brother came running towards him. They ran off to the barn and soon all the lambs were playing together. Limbo was happy but he knew Esha would come looking for him. He did not want to go back.

Later, when Esha realized that Limbo was missing, she ran out to search for him. Limbo saw her coming towards the barn. "Oh my, what should I do, what should I do," said Limbo.

Larky screamed, "Follow me, brother," and ran out to where the pigs were playing in the mud and they both jumped into it. Limbo pushed his head into the wet mud and covered his pink body with it too. Soon the other lambs also jumped into the mud. Dirty and covered in mud, they ran back to the barn just as Esha entered.

Lying under the straw hiding among the others Limbo was the dirtiest of them all. Esha pushed the lambs aside one by one to find her pink lamb with the heart-shaped mark on his forehead, but she couldn't find him. All of them looked the same. Sighing unhappily, she went running down to the lake to look for him. The lambs bleated happily.

Esha kept searching and searching but soon got very tired. There was no sign of Limbo. She sat down under the oak tree and heard her friend's voice calling out to her in the distance. "Tina, Tina. I am here," she said.

"What are you doing here?" Tina asked, walking up to her.

"Limbo has run away. I was looking for him. Please don't tell me again that I should not keep him as my pet," Esha said. They sat in silence for some time.

"Remember the time when I had been sent to town to look after my aunt?" Tina asked Esha.

"Of course, I do. I remember how worried I was wondering how you were doing. I thought you would never return. Thank goodness you came back home," said Esha.

Tina hugged her friend tightly and said, "What I never told you is how unhappy I was being away from my dearest friend. I still remember sitting in my room with no one to talk to or play with. Uncle asked me to make friends. The neighbour's daughter did not want to be my friend. I had never felt so lonely in my life. I missed the fresh air, the blue skies, this beautiful oak tree we are sitting under. Most of all, I missed you. Limbo too deserves to be out with his friends and family."

Esha sighed, "You are so right. I never realized how unhappy poor Limbo must have been. No wonder he ran away. I promise to take him back to his family. I can always play with him in the barn."

Esha walked back to the house and sat down on the swing in the garden. She began to cry when a soft nudge made her turn around. It was Limbo.

"Limbo, you are back," she cried and hugged him. Limbo wriggled out of her arms and ran to the house. She screamed with joy seeing all the other lambs on the porch and hugged them one by one feeling very happy.

"Go, Limbo. Go with your little friends. I will come to play with you in the barn," she said. Limbo bleated with joy and all the lambs followed him as they ran off together to play in the barn.

 Moral: Always pay attention to the feelings of another first rather than doing things just the way you want to do.

5

THE GRASSHOPPER AND THE BUTTERFLY

Hoppy, the grasshopper lived on a green plant among the beautiful roses, sunflowers and daisies growing in the garden. There was something different about Hoppy. One of her wings was dark green but the other was dark brown. Lacey the butterfly was her friend. Hoppy loved to disturb her by rubbing her back legs and snapping her wings.

Lacey was pink and black in colour but she would sit only on flowers that had a pleasant smell. Hoppy would jump from one plant to another looking for flowers for Lacey. Lacey laid her eggs on the undersides of the leaves of the cherry tree and they watched over them day and night.

One day, strong winds and raindrops hurt Lacey's wing and she fell sick. Hoppy realized that her best friend couldn't fly. "Don't feel sad," Hoppy said, "I am there for you. Remember the time when I was not well. You would tell me not to lose hope."

Hoppy took a small leaf and covered her with it. She watched over her friend for days, keeping her safe from other insects. Days passed and soon Lacey was well, but sadly she could never fly again.

"Oh Hoppy, who will play with you now? Go and find another friend to play with," said Lacey sadly.

Hoppy replied, "Don't say that, Lacey. Friends don't break their friendship just because they cannot play together."

As she said this, they heard noises. It was Lacey's children. The little ones came out from the chrysalis and said, "Mama!" Lacey smiled happily and said, "Hoppy, look you have new friends. Go and play with them. I will wait for you."

Hoppy rubbed her legs together and said, "Come on, little ones. Let's go and find some flowers for you". Lacey watched her friend hop from twig to twig with her baby butterflies flying around her.

Moral: Good friends will never leave you. They will always be with you in some way or the other.

6

THE FOREST ON THE OTHER SIDE

Piny, the rabbit, Monk, the monkey and Leo, the tiger, were best friends. In the forest where they lived, one day the pond completely dried up. The trees became bare and brown. There was no water to drink and no food to eat for the animals. The animals had a meeting and it was decided that they would send someone to look for a new place to stay.

Piny said to his two friends, "Let us go across the bridge to the other side of the forest and find some water and food. I am very thirsty and hungry."

"Good idea, but you know how old the bridge is. It will break if we try to cross it and we could fall into the valley below," said Leo.

"Even if we do, Mrs. Troll who is guarding it won't allow you to cross it," said Monk.

"Oh yes, I know," said Piny, "it is not only old but it is narrow also and leads straight into troll land, but I am too hungry to care."

"We can go one by one, but we will have to walk very slowly, "said Leo.

"So, who will go first?" asked Piny.

"Not I," said Monk.

"Not I," said Leo too.

Piny said, "Don't worry, I will go first. I am just a small rabbit. The bridge will not break under my weight. I will go and talk to the her."

Leo and Monk both agreed happily.

Piny stepped onto the bridge and began to hop across. As he was crossing the bridge, it started to shake. Piny was scared. He decided to talk to himself loudly as he slowly crossed the bridge, "Shaky, shake, shake. Over the bridge, I go. Trolls live there, I've been told. Shaky, shake, shake."

On the other side of the bridge, over the deep valley in troll land, Mrs. Troll blinked as she heard Piny talking. Mrs. Troll came rushing to the bridge and shouted, "Stop! Who dares to cross the bridge?"

Piny cried, "Oh, Mrs. Troll, it is me Piny. My friends and I want to cross the bridge to take food home for the others. Our forest has turned dry and there is no food left for us."

Mrs. Troll replied, "We are kind people and we have lots of food in our forest. Sure, Piny, you can cross the bridge, but I have two conditions. Our children have been lost in the mountains for days. You have to help us find them. The second condition is to help me repair the bridge because it will collapse before your friends cross over."

"What happened to the children?" Piny asked.

Mrs. Troll replied, "Four of the children went up the mountain to play and never came back. We searched for them, but all we heard was the scary wind and howling sounds. The children must be hiding in the caves, but there are wolves up there. We can't fight them. If you can help us find our children, then I will allow you all to cross over. If you want, you can also come and live in our forests."

Piny said, "Let me go back and bring my friends, I am sure they will agree to help." Piny went back and told his friends about Mr. Troll's conditions.

Monk asked Piny, "But how can we help?"

Piny replied, "It is simple. I am a good jumper and climber. Besides, I can hear sounds from a long way off which even trolls find difficult to hear. Leo, you have a powerful sense of smell and the wolves will be scared of you. Monk, you can climb high in the tree branches to guide us. So what do you say?"

Leo and Monk thought for a while. Leo said, "I think Piny is right, we should help them. If we help them, we will be able to help our other friends find a new home."

So one by one they crossed the shaky bridge. Leo said to Mrs. Troll, "I am ready to help you bring your children back and even build the bridge."

"Here, first have some water and food I have bought for you," said Mrs. Troll. When they were done eating, she said, "Now let's start building the bridge and making it stronger so that your friends can cross over without any fear."

Mrs. Troll started collecting fat branches from the tree. Piny trimmed the corners of the fat branches with his sharp teeth. With the help of their tails, Leo and Monk placed them on the bridge and Mrs. Troll tied them all together with some strong hanging roots of the tree. They made the bridge stronger using mud and leaves to fill the cracks. Soon the bridge was completed.

"Look", said Piny happily, "it no more goes shaky, shake, shake."

"Wow, well done," said Mrs. Troll, "and now it is time to keep your second promise before you bring your other animal friends to live here. Help me find our children."

Up the mountain went the three friends with the trolls following them. Monk leapt from one tree to another, shouting out directions to them. The wolves heard Leo roar and ran away with their tails between their legs.

It was not long before Leo said, "I smell children. They are hiding in that cave over there," and bounded inside.

The screams of the children became louder as they came running out screaming, "It's a tiger. It's a tiger." The trolls led out a loud cheer and hugged the missing children.

Mrs. Troll kept her promise and said, "Go and bring the rest of your animal friends to live in our forest." The three friends went back to lead all their friends, over the bridge to live happily in troll land.

Moral: When you work together, you can always make it happen.

7

RUDOLPH'S SHINY NOSE

It was a cold winter night. It was the day before Christmas. Everyone had finished decorating their Christmas trees and hanging up stockings. The bell in the tower was ringing and children were playing in the snow. It was getting colder and the fog was moving in. In a tiny house at the corner of the street, with its broken roof, lived Mama Helen and her children, Daisy and Jim. In their tiny broken down garden stood a snowman with a torn muffler around its neck. The fireplace in the house was silent.

Hungry and tired, the children asked, "Mama, do you think Santa will come this year?"

Mama Helen replied, "I don't know my children. I hope he does. I am going out to get some wood for the fire, so please just sleep. I will be back soon."

She hugged the children goodnight and went out. She looked up into the night sky and sighed, "Santa, if you really exist then please give me a Christmas miracle. I have no work and I am about to lose our home too. All I wish for is food and warm clothes to get my children through the winter." Unhappy and crying silent tears, she ran out into the forest to pick up sticks for the fire.

Far away in the North Pole, Santa pulled up his boots and heard Mama Helen cry. He smiled and said, "I will come, Mama Helen. I will." Santa quickly put on his red coat and hat, twirled his white moustache and said, "Come on Prancer, Dancer, Comet, Cupid, Donner, Dasher, Vixen, Blitzen and Rudolph. Get in line. It is time to go." He jumped into the sleigh and took off into the starry skies with a Ho, Ho, Ho. The sky was filled with sparkling stars and as the sleigh whizzed past, the stars waved and shone brighter. "Lead on, dear Rudolf, with your nose so bright. Won't you guide my sleigh tonight," laughed Santa.

Then it happened. Rudolf, the red-nosed reindeer, sneezed and the light of his nose went out. The sleigh came to a screeching stop. "Oh dear, this is a disaster," said Santa jumping out of the sleigh. He stood on the white carpet of clouds, wondering what to do. The other reindeers burst into laughter. They all gathered around Rudolf and slowly twisted his nose.

"Ouch, ouch, that hurts," cried Rudolph.

"Let me try to twist it again," Santa said, "Look, I did it. The light on his nose is shining again. Come on, Rudolph, let's be on our way."

Off went the sleigh into the sky and soon Santa reached the town and began climbing down the chimney. Slowly and quietly, he put all the gifts under the tree and off he went down another chimney, then another and again another. Santa's sleigh was way over the forest when it started to jerk. Then it happened again.

"Stop, stop, Santa. It is Rudolph. His nose has stopped shinning again," screamed Dasher.

Santa quickly steered the sleigh downwards and pulled it to a stop in front of the poorly dressed and shivering woman. Mama Helen dropped the sticks she had collected and froze in fright. "Don't be scared. I just need help, Mama Helen," said Santa.

Mama Helen gulped, "Is that really you, Santa? Oh my, you are real. What is wrong?" Santa told her what had happened and Mama Helen laughed. "Oh Santa, it must be a cold. I know how to cure it because my children get colds so often. Come with me," she said gathering up the sticks she had dropped.

Santa asked Rudolph to come with him and told the rest of the reindeer to stay hidden until he came back. He pulled out his bag of gifts from the sleigh and followed her. Mama Helen pushed the door open and quickly put the sticks into the fire. "Go and sit by the fire, Rudolph. Get warm. I will get some medicine for you and some hot tea for you too, Santa."

Hearing the noise, Daisy and Jim jumped out of bed and screamed in joy, "It's Santa. It's Santa."

Mama Helen applied some medicine on Rudolph's nose and rubbed it gently. Rudolph sneezed three times "Achoo, Achoo, Achoo", and it began to shine again. He smiled, "Look Santa, my nose is shining bright again. I am feeling better already."

"Take some of this medicine with you," said Mama Helen. Santa put the bottle in his coat's pocket and thanked her. He asked the children what they wanted for Christmas.

Daisy said, "If the roof got repaired, it would be great as it is too cold and please can Mama get her job back."

Jim said, "I want Rudolph to be my friend. Please, can he come and visit us every Christmas?" Rudolph rubbed his nose against Jim's shoulder and smiled at his new friend.

Santa promised that he would make it all happen. He pulled out some cake and biscuits from his bag and put them on the kitchen table. He sipped on the hot tea and watched the hungry children eat happily.

Then Santa insisted that they take out a gift each from his bag. Daisy pulled out a beautiful doll with a polka-dot dress and Jim got the red sports car he had always wanted. Mama Helen cried tears of joy as Santa placed a warm coat around her shivering shoulders. He put more gifts around their tiny tree and hugged the grateful Mama Helen saying, "I have to go now. It is getting late. There are lots of chimneys I need to climb down still."

"May we please see the other reindeer too, Santa?" asked Daisy. So they all walked back to the forest.

Rudolph said to the other reindeer, "Look my nose is shining bright again. It was just a cold. Mama Helen fixed it." He turned to Santa, "Santa, please can my new friends join us in the sleigh tonight".

"Jump in kids. You are coming with me today to distribute gifts. You too, Mama Helen," said Santa holding his hand out to help her climb into the sleigh.

Mama Helen laughed, "Thank you, Santa. I believe in you now and will always believe in the miracle of Christmas too." Off they went into the starry skies with a Ho, Ho, Ho.

Moral: If you are grateful for what you have, you will end up having more.

8

THE ONE-EYED SHARK AND THE OCTOPUS

Under the dark grey ocean lived a one-eyed shark called Sharky with a tail like a question mark. He had lost his eye while trying to save Fisho, the fish, from a wild shark. Sharky lived happily with the others in the deep waters of the ocean. Crabby, the crab, was his best friend.

Far away in another corner of the ocean, lived an old, mean and deadly octopus. He was called Shorthead because he had a small head and very long tentacles. He lived inside a sunken boat. Hiding in the crevice of the rocks near the sunken boat, he would grab the fish in his tentacles and eat them. He was very jealous of Sharky.

One day, Shorthead was sleeping peacefully when he heard loud splashing sounds. He opened one eye to see a baby fish swimming close and pretended to sleep. As soon as Fisho came close, he grabbed him in his tentacle. Just as he was about to eat him, Fisho cried out, "Wait, wait, Mr. Shorthead. Don't eat me. I am a deadly fish and you will die if you do. I have come to talk to you. I have an idea on how to bring the other fish to you so that you can eat them."

Shorthead laughed and asked, "How can you help me and why do you want to help me? You are so tiny."

Fisho said, "The other fish don't play with me and are always teasing me. Both of us are lonely and have no friends. I can help you. We need to teach them a lesson not to be mean to others." Shorthead asked, "What is your plan?"

Fisho smiled and said, "I will tell them that I have found a new place where there are lots of worms and plants for them to eat. I know they will be curious and will follow me. I will lead them to you." So Shorthead agreed to his plan.

The next day, Fisho swam up to the fishes playing and said, "Come with me, I have found a better place to eat." They laughed at him at first, but he convinced them and so they agreed to follow him.

Crabby watched them swim off and thought to himself, "Something is not right. Let me follow them." He followed them and suddenly saw lots of bubbles and heard noises. Frightened, he rushed back to bring Sharky.

Sharky said, "I will go and help them. You go and get more of your crab friends." He reached just in time as Shorthead was about to eat the fish. Sharky shouted, "Leave them alone, Shorthead. Don't you dare touch my friends. Go back to your sunken boat."

Shorthead grabbed Sharky's tail. Sharky got caught in the tentacle, unable to move. "How could you do this, Fisho? Have you forgotten that I lost my eye because of you. I never thought this is how you would repay me," said Sharky, "Do something. Help me."

Fisho felt ashamed but he knew that he could not fight the octopus.

As they were all struggling to escape, Crabby and his friends arrived. They started snapping at the octopus.

Shorthead cried out in pain, "Stop, stop, you are hurting me," but the crabs kept going snap, snap,

snap at his tentacles. One by one, Shorthead let the fishes go and soon Sharky was free too.

Shorthead began to cry, "I am not going to live here anymore. No one wants to be my friend. All of you are mean and make fun of me all the time, just because I am old now. One day Sharky is going to eat you all up like I was. Just wait and see."

Sharky said, "I will never do that and there is no need for you to run away too. We are sorry and I promise that no one will make fun of you again. We will get food for you so that you won't go hungry. Please don't go." Shorthead stopped crying and soon the ocean was filled with sounds of laughter.

Moral: Remember that there is always someone worse off than yourself. Put yourself in someone else's shoes to see how they feel.

9

THE MAGIC SCHOOL BAG

In a village lived three best friends, who would go to school together every day. Rinku was a tall boy with dark brown eyes and loved to eat. Tinku loved sports and hated school, and Minku loved to sleep. Every day they would get late for school. They would wander in the forest on the way, play by the lake and throw stones into it. They told the teacher a new lie every day.

Tinku would say that he had got up early but had to help his mother with the housework. Rinku lied that he had to catch two buses to reach the school and the bus was never on time. Minku said that he was having trouble getting up early. This went on for many days and each time the teacher forgave them.

One day, while coming back from school, they were surprised to see a new shop in the market. "What is this new shop, Rajaram's Bags and Belts," said Rinku, "I have never seen it before and look at that red coloured bag with black straps lying on the counter."

Tinku asked the shopkeeper to sell the bag to him. The shopkeeper offered the bag for free.

"Free," said Rinku, "then it is mine because I saw it first."

Tinku argued, "No it is not, because I asked for it from the shopkeeper."

The boys argued about who should get the bag. The shopkeeper stopped them and said, "Why are you fighting over the bag. Tinku, you take it but be careful with it."

Now Tinku became suspicious and asked, "Why are you giving it to me for free? No one gives anything for free."

Rajaram smiled and said, "Oh, don't be so suspicious. I am just being generous today because it is my birthday. I wanted to do something nice and you asked for the bag. So I thought why not give it to you."

Minku and Rinku were very unhappy so Rajaram said, "Don't be so unhappy. Here take these leather pencil boxes." The boys jumped in joy, wished him and left the shop happy.

Tinku showed the bag to his mother. His mother was very angry and asked him to return it. So he stuffed it inside his school bag and promised to return it.

Rinku's mother grabbed the leather pencil box and threw it in the dustbin and said, "Never take anything from strangers." Rinku quietly took it out from the dustbin and hid it. Minku hid the pouch in the drawer.

The next morning, as Tinku walked towards the lake to meet his friends, he felt like something was moving in his bag. Scared, he dropped his bag to the ground and opened it. Out popped the red bag and turned into a cycle in front of his eyes. He stared at it as the cycle circled around him. He quickly got on and just as he reached the big tree near the school gate, the cycle turned into the bag again. Tinku fell to the ground. He laughed, "That's funny," and stuffed the red bag into his school bag and walked to class. The teacher was very happy to see him reach in time.

Minku and Rinku were late as usual. Angry with Tinku for not meeting them at the lake, Minku asked, "Where were you? We were waiting for you. Just because of you we are late again. How did you reach in time?"

Tinku said, "Oh sorry, I forgot to tell you. I have a cycle now. My uncle has bought it for me. Don't wait for me from tomorrow."

The school bell rang. Leaving his friends behind, Tinku ran off to a deserted spot behind the school and took out the red bag. Once again it turned into a cycle. Tinku rode off and suddenly he fell on the ground close to his house as the cycle turned back into the red bag again. "Ouch, that hurt. Who wants a bag that keeps turning into a cycle? Why can't it just remain a cycle," he thought.

The next day, the two friends followed him after school. They knew he was hiding something. They saw Tinku waiting for all the children to leave the school ground. He pulled out the red bag and they watched as the bag turned into a cycle. Before he could ride off, they grabbed Tinku's cycle.

"So this is what you are hiding from us. It is the bag the shopkeeper gave you. How could you be so selfish? You could have told us."

The boys began to fight among themselves as the cycle kept circling them, it's silver bell ringing loudly.

"Stop circling and making noise. The teacher is still in the classroom. She will see you. Turn back into the bag before anyone comes," said Tinku to the cycle.

The cycle fell to the ground and turned back into the bag. The boys sat down next to it and Tinku said, "Look, this cycle is not so nice. It scares me. I miss walking to school with you. Anyway, I was going to return it to the shopkeeper today. We should just go and return this bag."

Suddenly, out popped a rope from the bag and tied the boys together. They screamed for help. The teacher heard them and came running out and untied them. Tinku told her the whole story but she laughed, "I don't believe this rope is magical. Are you trying to tell me that the bag turned into a cycle and now a rope? You are again making excuses and telling lies."

"No, teacher. This time we are telling the truth. Please believe us," cried the three boys.

"Okay then take me to the shop. I want to talk to the shopkeeper," said the teacher. She picked up the rope and they walked to the market. They looked for the shop but they could not find it.

Minku cried, "It was here, teacher. I promise the shop was here." The other shopkeepers said that they knew nothing about Rajaram's shop and no one had even heard about him. The boys were scared now as the shop seemed to have disappeared and no one was believing them.

The teacher threw the rope away and said, "This is all your imagination. You deserve to be punished for lying. Come on now, just go home."

Tinku quietly picked up the rope and hid it under his shirt and told his friends, "Come, let us go to my house and tell my father. He will believe us."

Tinku told his father the truth, but he also did not believe him. The father said, "You boys tell too many lies. How can I believe you? Just throw it away." The boys were sad and Tinku threw the rope out of the window. Suddenly, there was a knock at the door and when father opened the door, he was shocked to see a red bag floating in the air and then turn into a cycle and pedal off towards the old man walking down the path to the house. It was Rajaram.

"Look, father, this is the man who gave me the bag," Tinku said.

Rajaram smiled, "Yes, I am the one who gave your son the magic bag. It grants wishes and Tinku wished every night that he could sleep longer, play in the forest and magically reach school in time too. So it would turn into a cycle."

"Why did it turn in a rope then?" asked the father. Rajaram laughed and said, "It decides what to turn into on its own. I had given the other boys magic pencil boxes, but they never used them. They too could have got cycles. I just wanted them to be happy."

"Please take it away. This is not a wish coming true. I don't want a bag that keeps turning into a cycle or a rope whenever it wants. I have learnt my lesson. I promise never to be late to school," Tinku said. The three friends returned the gifts and were never late to school again.

Moral: Do not make wishes that are wrong for you.

10

THE HUNGRY BEAR AND THE BEEHIVE

Once a brown bear came to live under a big tree. The tree had a big honeycomb hanging on one of the branches. The bear was waiting for the bees to make the honey so that he could eat it. Days had passed and he was getting tired of waiting. One day, when

he was fast asleep under the tree, and started to snore very loudly. His snoring disturbed the little bee.
The little bee looked at the sleeping bear and said, "Look at the bear snoring, Mama. We need to do something or he will break our home."

"Leave him alone. He cannot harm us. We will sting him if he tries," said Mama Bee. The little bee was not happy and so he popped out from the honeycomb and buzzed around the bear. He began to irritate the bear and started singing,

"I am a honey bee.
My home is on this tree
I really do believe
Mr. Bear, that you should leave
Or I will sing my buzzing song
In your ear, all day long
Buzz, buzz, buzz."

The bear opened one eye and tried to brush it away, but the little bee did not stop buzzing in his ear. The bear got annoyed and woke up. "Stop! You are disturbing my sleep. Go away!" He swung his paw at the little bee. The little bee went crying to his mother.

Mama Bee flew down and settled on his nose and stung him. "Ouch, that hurt," said the bear. She looked him in the eye and said, "I know that you have made this your home, but we also live in the tree. If you touch our home or disturb us, we will sting you."

The bear said, "But I am a bear and I eat honey, so let's make a deal. You give me some honey and I will not touch your honeycomb. Just let me sleep peacefully here until then."

Mama Bee agreed to give him some honey and the bees never troubled him when he was sleeping.

One afternoon, the little bee was feeling bored. He buzzed off quietly into the bushes to suck some nectar from the flowers without disturbing the bear. Suddenly there was a loud sound.

The bear blinked and sighed, "Those naughty bees will never stop troubling me." He rolled over and went back to sleep.

It was not the bees, but a hunter who was hiding in the bushes to kill the bear. The little bee saw the hunter and started buzzing around him. The hunter hit him with a stick. The little bee lay stunned for a few moments, but he knew that he had to warn the bear.

So he began buzzing in the bear's ears. "Wake up, wake up, you silly bear or you will be killed," he buzzed, but the bear was fast asleep and did not hear him.

The hunter pointed the gun at the bear and aimed to fire. "Leave him alone," said the little bee and stung the hunter on his nose. The gun fell to the ground with a loud bang.

The bear woke up in a fright, growled in anger and hit the trunk of the tree so hard that the honeycomb fell to the ground. It broke into two pieces and all the bees come out of their home buzzing unhappily. Seeing the bear surrounded by the bees, the hunter ran away.

"Look what you did, you silly bear. You broke our home," said Mama Bee.

"I am sorry. I am sorry," cried the bear, "the sound of the gun frightened me. I did not mean to break your home. I will help you build it again."

Mama Bee laughed, "You can't build a honeycomb, silly bear. I know you did not mean to break it. No one can do anything now. You just go ahead and eat all the honey you want from our old home. Don't worry it won't take us long to build a new one." She turned to her bee troops and said, "Come. Let us build a new home."

The bees buzzed around her and set out to build a new home for the swarm to move into.

The bear smiled and sat down and licked the tasty honey from the broken honeycomb, "Yummy, yummy. It is so tasty," he said.

The little bee sat on the bear's nose. "Hi, little one. You are a good friend. You saved my life. I will be careful not to harm your home ever again. I promise," said the bear.

The little bee smiled and started to sing,

> "I am your friend, a honey bee
> My home is now on that tree
> And now I believe
> Mr. Bear, you shouldn't leave
> I will sing my buzzing song
> We will play all day long
> Buzz, buzz, buzz."

They watched the other bees buzzing around and building a new home and laughed.

Moral: All of our actions, no matter how small can help someone.

11

WHO IS BETTER - WIND OR WATER?

High in the sky among the clouds there lived Mr. Wind. He was very strong and he often blew hard on his friend, Mr. Water. Mr. Water would ripple and feel very tickled. The friends would laugh, blow and flow together. One fine day, they got into an argument.

Mr. Water said, "Do you know, Mr. Wind, how important I am? People use me to clean themselves and even play with me. I am very useful in the summer when people are thirsty. They need me every day too."

Mr. Wind replied, "Oh that is nothing. If people wash themselves, then they need me to dry off. I am so powerful that I can carry seeds to different parts of the earth to grow. People use me to make electricity. I can move at different speeds and in all different directions. You can't flow free. I am much cooler than you are."

"So what if I flow in one direction but if you help carry seeds, I water them so that they grow. I am more important than you are," argued Mr. Water.

They continued to argue and decided to test who is more important to people. They saw a little boy coming towards the river. Tired, Aarav sat down under the tree, opened his bottle and drank water. He was feeling still thirsty, so he walked to the river, filled his bottle, gulped down the cold water and sat down to rest.

Mr. Water said to Mr. Wind, "See how I helped him to quench his thirst."

Mr. Wind said, "That is fine but what would he have done if there was no river close by. Now, look at what I can do." Mr. Wind blew gently and it was so cooling that Aarav fell asleep peacefully.

They began to argue again. Mr. River swelled in anger and Mr. Wind whipped up a cyclone. The leaves of the tree fell on the ground near the boy's feet. Aarav woke up in fright and screamed, holding on tight to the tree.

"What is happening? Why is the water rising and why is there is such a strong wind? I hate the water and the wind," he said as he watched his bottle and his bag being dragged away by the wind and fall into the river. "Stop, stop. I am scared," said Aarav.

Hearing Aarav cry, Mr. Water and Mr. Wind stopped arguing and slowly the water and the wind calmed down. Aarav ran to the river to look for his things and cried, "No one will believe what happened. Mummy is going to be mad at me for losing my things. What am I going to do?"

They felt sorry for him and Mr. River said, "Quick, Mr. Wind, create a whirlpool in the water so that I can throw the bottle and the bag out to the boy." Mr. Wind stirred up the water and out popped the bottle and the bag and floated towards the surprised boy. Aarav picked them up and ran away.

"How silly can we be. Both of us are needed in our own way, so I think we should stop arguing about who is more important," said Mr. River. Both of them promised never to argue again and continued on their way happily.

Moral: Everyone has a place in the world. Everyone is important in their own way.

12

THE GRASSHOPPER AND THE MUSHROOM

There was a grasshopper named Nibbly, who was very hardworking. He lived under the peepal tree in the forest with his three friends, Snailo, the snail, Froggy, the frog and Sluggy, the slug. Hiding under a big leaf in the heavy rain with Nibbly, Sluggy grumbled, "Nibbly, why does the rain make the ground so slushy. I get all muddy and stuck. This leaf is also not helping us hide from the rain either."

Nibbly sighed, "You are a slug, but I am a grasshopper. I should be grumbling because the rain will wash me away." They both watched Snailo and Froggy frolicking in the rain. Nibbly decided to go and find something better for him and Sluggy to hide from the rain.

The next day Nibbly set off on his adventure. Wet and tired, he soon stopped to rest and fell asleep. It started to rain and Nibbly woke up with a start and realized that he was completely dry. He looked up and saw a huge red mushroom covering him like an umbrella. "Wow, what a beautiful mushroom. I am sure this mushroom will be useful for Sluggy and me to hide from the rains. I think I should take this mushroom back home, but how do I carry it?"

All of a sudden he heard a voice, "Of course you can take me with you." Nibbly looked around to see where the voice came from. The mushroom bent down and smiled at the shocked grasshopper.

Nibbly asked, "If I pull you out won't you die?"

"No," said the mushroom, "I can be pulled out and re-grown again. Besides, the rain will help more of us grow too."

A big black cat with a long tail hiding in the tree jumped down and smiled at the grasshopper and said, "Let me help you pull the mushroom out."

The cat twisted its tail around the mushroom and pulled it out and put it on the rock. "Hey, Mr. Cat, can you help me roll the rock all the way home," asked Nibbly. "I will do better than that. Let me help you. Jump onto my back and I will take you home," said Mr. Cat.

In the distance, the three friends saw a big cat with a giant mushroom in his tail coming towards them. Frightened, they ran helter-skelter and hid. Froggy peeped out from behind the tree and said to Sluggy, "Look, it is Nibbly."

"Woah, Woah," said Nibbly and jumped off the cat's back.

The mushroom said, "Put me down, Mr. Cat. Plant me quickly under the tree." Mr. Cat dug a hole under the tree and put the mushroom into it. They patted the mud all around it. All of them gathered around the mushroom.

Nibbly said, "Thank you, Mr. Mushroom and Mr. Cat for helping us." The mushroom bowed his head and smiled.

Soon more mushrooms sprouted around the big red mushroom. Sluggy and Nibbly never had to worry about where to hide in the rains anymore.

Moral: There is always a way out.

13

THE WITCH'S CURSE

Once there was a witch who lived in a hut at the edge of the forest. She was scary and mean. She was always troubling the villagers by turning them into rabbits, just for fun. She would take the rabbits to her house and wait for someone to come looking for them. No one came looking, so the next day she would turn them back to people.

Roohi and Ayanna were best friends. They often went to the forest to play on the wooden swing hanging from the huge tree. One sunny afternoon, the witch was hiding in the bushes and watched them play.

She went up to them and said, "Hello, little girls, I have come from the other side of the village. I am an old lady and I don't have friends. I see you both playing together every day. Seems that you both are best friends. May I join you?"

She looked strange so they said, "No, please, we are happy playing among ourselves. You are too old anyways to play with us."

The witch said, "I will turn you into a rabbit if you refuse." Roohi laughed, "Don't be funny. You do not have magical powers, so please just go away."

"Of course, I do. I am a witch," she smiled wickedly and turned Roohi into a rabbit.

Before the witch could grab the rabbit, Ayanna picked up Roohi in her arms and ran away crying,

"Help, Help me. The witch has turned my friend into a rabbit."

She ran as fast as she could and then suddenly stopped, "What have I done, what have I done. I should have let her take you, Roohi. She would have turned you back into a girl again tomorrow. Now you are going to remain a rabbit forever. No one will believe what happened." cried Ayanna hugging Roohi.

All of sudden, Roohi spoke and said, "Don't cry. It is not your fault. Let us go and find the witch and ask her to turn me back into a girl."

It had become dark and the parents were wondering where the girls had disappeared to. They gathered the villagers and decided to go look for the girls.

Ayanna was scared as she walked along the dark path in the forest. She saw an old man sitting under a tree. The old man was surprised to see a little girl holding a rabbit in her hand. "What are you doing in the forest at this time of the night," he asked.

Ayanna replied, "I am looking for the witch. She has turned my friend into a rabbit. I need to find her."

The old man said, "Oh dear. I know where she lives."

Ayanna said, "Please can you take me to her house?"

The old man was scared to go with her but told her how to get there. "Follow this path till you reach a pond. Cross over to the other side and you will see a small hut with smoke coming out of the chimney. That is where you will find the witch." Ayanna thanked the old man and continued walking. Soon she saw the hut in the distance.

Roohi said to Ayanna, "Let me go inside alone. I will trouble her so much that she will turn me back into a girl. You hide till I am back. Push me in through that window."

Ayanna pushed Roohi through the window. Roohi dropped to the ground and saw that the witch was sleeping. She jumped on her. The witch woke up with a start and saw a rabbit sitting on the bed. Roohi jumped off the bed and hopped around breaking things.

The witch picked up her broom and started whacking the rabbit, "Why are you troubling me. Who are you and what do you want?"

Roohi said, "I am Roohi. You have turned me into a rabbit. Turn me back otherwise I will keep breaking things."

The witch was angry now. "I will turn you into a stone rabbit. You will never be a girl again," she screamed.

Just as the witch began casting a spell, Ayanna ran into the room and picked up Roohi in her arms and said, "Don't you dare hurt my friend. Turn her back into a girl right now!"

The witch looked at the two friends and laughed. She turned the rabbit back into a girl. The girls were so happy that they hugged the witch tight and said, "Thank you. Thank you."

The witch was surprised. "You hugged me. How can you bear to touch me?" she asked. As she said this she turned into a little girl. "Look, I am a girl again. Thank you so much for breaking the spell," she said, "I am Veda. I was an orphan and the ugliest girl in the village. No one liked me so I got so angry. I started harassing everyone and stealing from the villagers. One day, I stole from the old witch living in this house. She caught me and turned me into a witch. Only true friendship will turn you back into a girl, she had said."

Ayanna asked, "Is that why you turned my friend into a rabbit?"

Veda replied, "I turned one friend into a rabbit hoping that the other friend would come looking for them. No one came but you."

The villagers were surprised to see three girls in the witch's hut. They asked, "Where is the witch?" Ayanna pointed to Veda, "There she is." The villagers were shocked. When they heard her story, Ayanna's mother asked Veda to come and live with them. Veda was happy. The girls returned home with the villagers.

Moral: Be a good friend in good times and bad. A good friend is someone who always watches out for you.

14

MR. SUN AND HIS PLANET FRIENDS

Once upon a time, high up in an empty dark galaxy, there lived a round and yellow ball of fire named Mr. Sun. He passed his time watching the stardust twirl and dance in changing patterns, but he was very unhappy. He was all alone so he laid around in the darkness with his golden rays flickering sadly. Mr. Sun said, "If only I could get to meet God one day, then I could ask him to help me find friends and shine bright again?"

Suddenly lightning struck. It flashed four times and stopped. Mr. Sun thought to himself, "Hmmm, this is very strange," and then he heard a voice. He opened his weary eyes and saw God dressed in white flowing robes, riding on a chariot flying towards him, lighting up the dark skies.

God said, "You wanted to meet me so here I am. Nice to see you. What do you want from me?"

Mr. Sun cried, "I am lonely." God smiled, "Don't worry and come with me. You won't be alone anymore and you will make a lot of friends".

Mr. Sun glowed, "Please, dear God, please take me there." God held out his hand and they whizzed off. Off they went, leaving flashes of fire and lightning dancing behind them. "Where are we going?" asked Mr. Sun just as they flew into a circle of dark planets spinning around in the distance.

God stopped and laughed as Mr. Sun spun around like a top a few times dizzy from the flying. "Meet your new friends, Mr. Sun. They are lonely too. I will bring all of you together to live in the galaxy and you will be their leader," said God. All the planets shouted with joy.

God ordered all the planets to stand in line. Tapping the planet closest to him, God started naming them one by one. He called them Mercury, Venus, Earth, Mars, Jupiter, Saturn, Uranus and Neptune.

"So that is done and now all that is left is to give your special places. All of you will spin around Mr. Sun in an anti-clockwise direction," said God.

God moved around the planets and started to arrange them around Mr. Sun. The planets began to glow with the light of Mr. Sun.

Venus said, "Dear God, look I am the hottest and brightest one now. I want to be closest to Mr. Sun."

Mercury argued, "But I want to be close to Mr. Sun."

They started to fight. Mr. Sun stopped them and said, "Why are you making so much noise? Let God decide what is best for you."

God decided, "Mercury will be closest to Mr. Sun and Venus will be second. Now, who wants to be next to Venus?"

Mother Earth said, "I would love to be a little away from Mr. Sun. Too much of his hot rays may destroy my people and plants." Mars begged, "I would be happy to be close to Mother Earth."

Saturn turned to Jupiter and said, "my dear friend Jupiter, I have rings filled with dust and ice pieces and I tilt too, so let me be far from you so that my rings don't hurt you."

"Okay," said God, "it is good that you both have decided your places without fighting. So, Mr. Sun, who is left now?"

Uranus and Neptune both spoke up together, "Dear God and Mr. Sun, we both are left."

Uranus said to God, "I want to be far away from Mr. Sun. I want to be the coldest one."

Neptune said, "I would love to be next to Uranus because I have too many storms in my atmosphere. I too want to remain the coldest of all."

"So we are all done," said God, when a meek voice piped up. "You forgot about me." God smiled at the shiny Moon and said, "You are special. You will revolve around Mother Earth and shine your silvery light on her."

God clapped his hands and asked the planets to fall into their places, "Are you happy now, Mr. Sun. Would you like to live here with them?"
Mr. Sun smiled and said, "Yes, please. I want to live here with all my planet friends. Now I will never be lonely anymore." From that day onwards, Mr. Sun was never sad again.

Moral: God has a plan for each one of us better than what we can ever make for ourselves.

15

CHOCOLATES FROM THE SKY

It was a cloudy day and there was a sweet smell of grass and the birds were chattering in the trees. Aarav and Kian, two mischievous brothers, were busy playing in their secret hideout in the hollow of a tree in the forest. Ramu, the watchman's son hid in the bushes and watched them play.

Suddenly, a bird peeped into the tree trunk. "Shoo, shoo," said Aarav and as they watched it fly they saw something falling from the sky.

They jumped out of their hideout and looked up at the sky. The sky was green in colour and there was a green cloud floating with fruit and chocolates falling from it. They grabbed all the chocolates that they could. Ramu rushed out of his hiding place, but they pushed him away when he tried to take some.

"Go away, you dirty boy. Where did you come from? These are for us. You can't take them." Ramu was sad and watched them fill their pockets with fruits and chocolates.

Then something funny happened. Every time Kian picked up a chocolate, it vanished.

Kian said, "How funny is that. These are not real fruits or chocolates. Aarav, let us forget about it. Let us go."

They climbed high up on the tree to see whether they could touch the green cloud, but it was not possible. Two beautiful birds flew down out from the green cloud and sat on the branch and said, "Hello children, we are birds from the green sky. Would you like to take a ride and eat all the fruit and chocolates you can?"

The boys were eager to know why a part of the sky was green and why fruits and chocolates were falling from the sky, so they agreed.

Ramu said, "Please, take me along with you," but the boys said, "Stop following us. We don't like you. Can't you see there are only two birds?"

They climbed onto the backs of the birds. The birds flapped their wings and flew off into the green sky. Ramu watched sadly as the two boys flew away.

Finally, the birds stopped and the boys jumped off on a carpet of clouds. The boys were surprised to see lots of huge trees with fruits and chocolates hanging from the branches. There were nests on the trees with all kinds of colourful birds and they all spoke. Kian asked the birds why the sky looked green.

Big Bird replied, "It is the glow from the trees and grass. Many years ago our homes got burnt in a forest fire. We were flying around looking for a place to stay when a green light shone on us and we flew into it up to the sky above. We made this our home. We wanted to share the goodies with you so we decided to drop some on the ground below."

The boys smiled and began to fill the basket with fruits and chocolates from the trees. Then it happened again. Every time they put something in the basket, it vanished.

Aarav was surprised and asked Big Bird, "What is happening? Why are the goodies vanishing again? Why can't we fill the basket?"

Big Bird replied, "You are ungrateful and selfish children. You never shared the chocolates with Ramu. That is why you will not get any."

Kian said, "We promise to share the goodies with Ramu when we go back. We will also share it with the other children." Soon they were able to fill the baskets with fruits and chocolates.

"Let's get back now. Remember to share the goodies," said Big Bird. The boys climbed onto the birds' backs and were dropped off in the forest. They ran home with the baskets.

The next day, Aarav and Kian shared the goodies with Ramu and the other poor children. Ramu was now their best friend. From that day onwards, Big Bird came to meet the three boys every time they went to the forest. The three boys would collect the goodies and distribute them among the other children every time. It was their secret and no one else ever came to know.

Moral: Be generous. Sharing is caring and it makes you feel good.

16

THE TALKING TREES

Far away in the jungle, a monkey was swinging from the trees when he heard the other monkeys talk among themselves. Curious, he went closer and heard them say, "Have you heard about the talking tree that fulfils wishes and asks for something in return? If you don't give something, then the tree pulls you into the branches and keeps you inside it forever."

The monkey told this to the birds on the trees. The birds went and whispered it to the other animals in the jungle.

The wolf laughed, "What rubbish! A tree that fulfills wishes."

The elephant said, "Deep in the forest I have often heard the crackling and snapping of the tree branches at night. I never go there."

"What if the bird is right and wishes are granted. Do you not want a wish?" asked the cat.

The tiger said, "It could just be the hunters hiding so how about sending that foolish donkey first. We can hide and watch what happens."

"I am not afraid," said the donkey, "I am going to look for the tree. Come if you want."

So the other animals followed him. When they reached there, they saw a circle of trees all looking the same. The trees were huge with hanging roots dipping into the ground with twisted branches like fingers. The animals looked at them and wondered.

The wolf said, "There are so many trees. Which one is the talking tree and are you sure that it will grant us wishes."

The donkey said, "Hee-haw. Hee-haw. Wow, what lovely trees. I heard that one of you talks. Which one of you talks? So, let's hear you talk." But no one answered. Once again the donkey brayed loudly, going hee-haw, hee-haw, but still no one spoke.

Fed up, the other animals told him, "Stop being foolish and stop that horrible noise. This is not a magical place. Let us go home."

Hearing this, one of the trees started to talk, "Donkey, why are you wasting time talking nonsense? Do you want a wish or not? Stop that awful noise and just ask for one."

The donkey smiled and said, "Make me the king of the jungle."

The tree laughed and pulled him into the branches. "Help, help!"cried the donkey.

Suddenly, the other trees came alive and spread their branches to catch the other animals. The branches crashed against each other like loud thunder as the animals began to run helter-skelter trying to escape. One by one the trees caught the animals and pulled them into their branches.

The elephant was too big for the trees to catch and so he ran around shaking the trees and breaking the branches to free the other animals. "Leave my friends alone or I will uproot you," said the elephant.

"Please stop breaking us. We are so sorry for hurting your friends," the trees begged the elephant. One by one the animals dropped down from the branches. Soon all the animals were free.

The elephant asked, "Why did you pull my friends into your branches?"

The tree replied, "Every night people came with axes and cut us down. They could never hear us talk and so we did not know what to do. If we caught them in our branches, they would cut it off. So we would catch the animals in our branches to protect us. When the people came, we would just free the animals and they would run away frightened."

The tiger said, "We will help you. Every night, some of us will come and stay with you." The animals protected them every night and the trees never had to worry about the people hurting them.

Moral: It is up to each of us to care for others around us.

17

THE ALIEN COW

Out in the woods, on a run-down farm, lived an old farmer with his wife. The farm was once full of animals but now all the farmer had was a cow, a dog, a rabbit and a horse. The cow and the horse lived in the old barn with half-open doors. The dog and rabbit slept on the hay in the barn. The farmer never gave them names so they decided to name themselves. "Let us name ourselves after a letter. When we grow old, we may not remember the names. I will be H for horse," said the horse. So they named themselves H, R and C and D. Days went by and they were happy together.

Late one night, high up in the sky, a space ship ran out of fuel. The wind started blowing fiercely as it fell to the earth. H looked up at the sky and thought he saw a flash of light. He was sure that far away in the forest something had fallen from the sky. He woke his friends up and they ran to find out more. They stared at the spaceship among the trees and D said, "Don't go too close. We don't even know what sort of creatures live inside. What if they try to eat us?" The door of the spaceship opened. A purple polka-dotted two-headed cow and four tails came out.

C looked at the alien cow in shock and said, "Are you a cow? You look just like me but you have two heads and more tails."

H asked, "What brings you here?"

The alien cow replied, "Fear not friends, I come in peace. I was on my way to my planet when the engine of my spaceship stopped working. Will you help me, please?"

"How can we help? We know nothing about repairing spaceships," said R.

Before the alien cow could stop him, D ran inside the spaceship saying, "Let me check what is wrong."

He pressed a few buttons and suddenly the engine started to work, the door closed and the spaceship took off.

The alien cow screamed in anger as he watched his spaceship fly out into the sky. R shouted at him, "You are such a liar. See, your spaceship is working fine. Bring my friend back at once."

"Stop hitting me, you stupid rabbit. Why will I want to land here and let you all see me? I don't know how he did that. Let me call my friend Rambo to bring him back," cried the alien cow.

The alien cow pulled out one of its tails and started talking into it.

H said, "Ouch, doesn't that hurt. You crazy alien cow."

The alien cow laughed, "Not at all. It is my device to talk to other spaceships."

He called his friend, Rambo. "Come in, Rambo. I am stuck on earth and a stupid dog has stowed away in my spaceship. He is flying around somewhere up there. Find him and get him back to me," said the alien cow.

Rambo replied, "Don't worry. Leave it to me. I will find him."

Rambo soon found the lost spaceship and saw the dog stuck inside. D was frightened as he watched the spaceship fly close. "Oh my! More aliens! How am I going to get back? Can anyone hear me? Someone help me! I want to go home."

Rambo said, "Don't cry. I have come to help you."
Rambo pulled out one of his tails and caught the
spaceship with it and dragged it back to earth. The
spaceship landed on the ground and D came running
out of it happy. H, R and C hugged him tight and
jumped around in joy.

The alien cow asked, "How did you get the spaceship
to start?"

D said, "The green button seemed to be jammed. I
just pulled it." They all laughed.

The alien cow turned to C and said, "You are so
much like us. Would you like to come and live with
us."

C replied, "I would love to come but I am not exactly
like you. This is my home and these are my friends.
I am happy here with them. You can always come
and visit us."

So the alien cow gave one of his tails to C and said, "Take this, so that you can stay in touch with us."

"How funny is that," said C, "your tails have so many uses. All I do is use it as a fly swatter."

The alien cow and Rambo waved goodbye to the friends promising to return soon. The friends watched them fly away.

Moral: You do not leave your friends and family behind no matter what.